Old Mother Hubbard

Illustrated by

Aurelius Battaglia

W9-CDD-972

A GOLDEN BOOK • New York
Western Publishing Company, Inc.
Racine, Wisconsin 53404

Copyright © 1970 by Western Publishing Company, Inc. All rights reserved. Printed in the U.S.A. No part of this book may be reproduced or copied in any form without written permission from the publisher. GOLDEN®, GOLDEN & DESIGN®, A LITTLE GOLDEN BOOK®, and A GOLDEN BOOK® are trademarks of Western Publishing Company, Inc. ISBN 0-307-02136-X QRST

Old Mother Hubbard
Went to the cupboard,
To get her poor dog a bone;
When she got there
The cupboard was bare,
And so the poor dog had none.

She went to the baker's
To buy him some bread,

But when she came back
The poor dog was dead.

She went to the joiner's
To buy him a coffin,

But when she came back
The poor dog was laughing.

She took a clean dish
To get him some tripe,

But when she came back
He was smoking his pipe.

She went to the fishmonger's
To buy him some fish,

But when she came back
He was licking the dish.

She went to the hatter's
To buy him a hat,

But when she came back
He was feeding the cat.

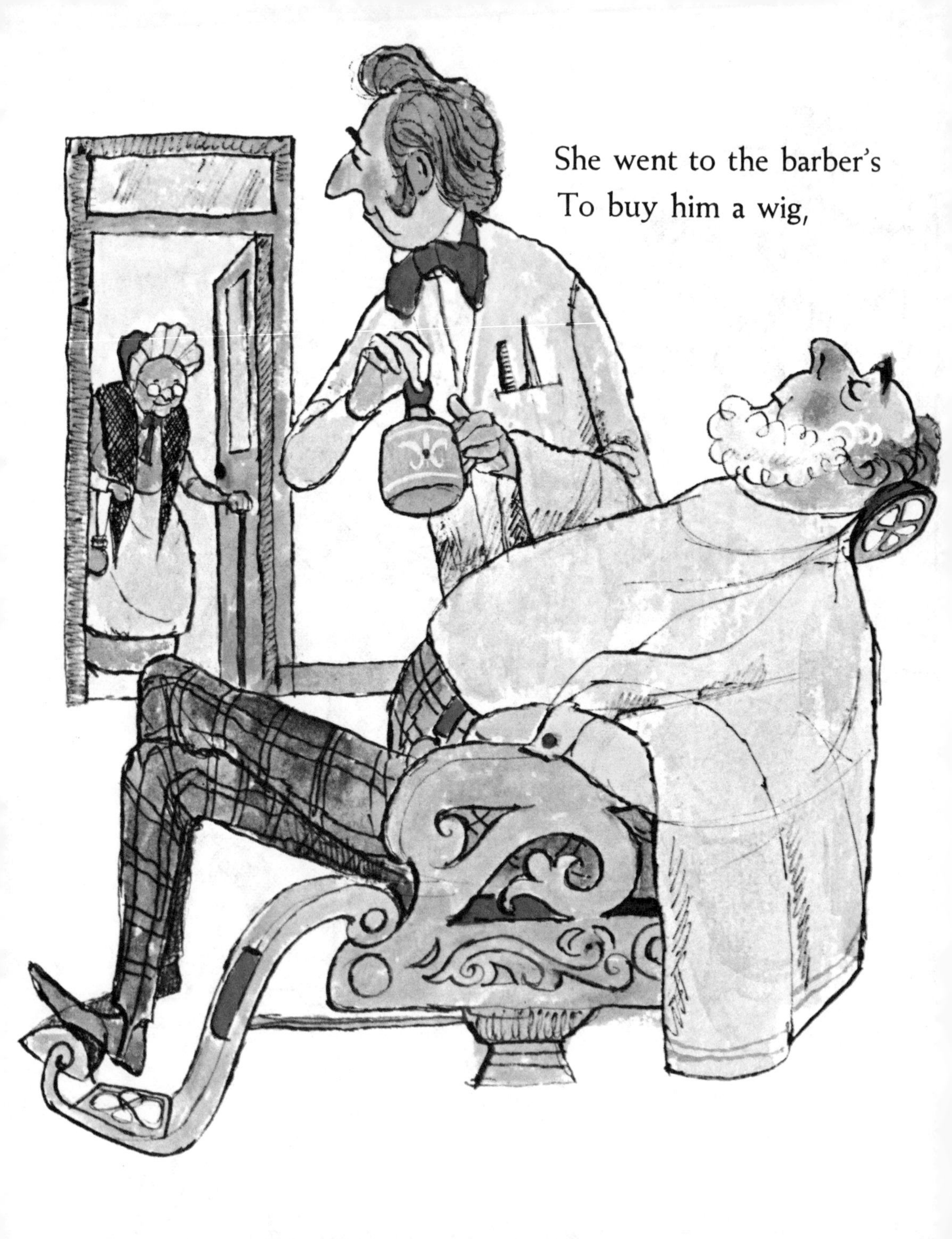

She went to the barber's
To buy him a wig,

But when she came back
He was dancing a jig.

She went to the grocer's
To buy him some fruit,

But when she came back
He was playing the flute.

She went to the tailor's
To buy him a coat,

But when she came back
He was riding a goat.

She went to the cobbler's
To buy him some shoes,

But when she came back
He was reading the news.

She went to the sempstress
To buy him some linen,
But when she came back
The dog was spinning.

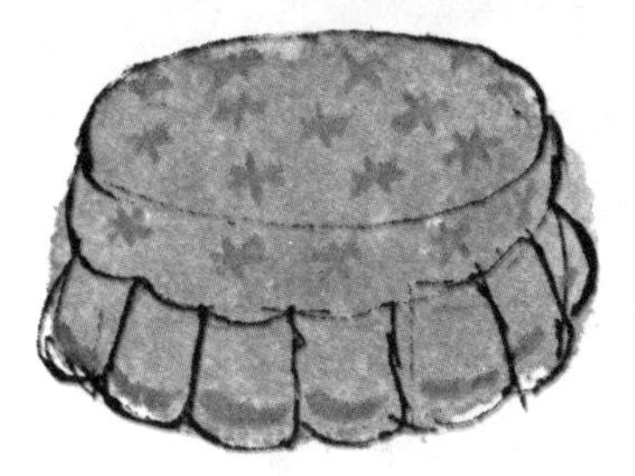

She went to the hosier's
To buy him some hose,
But when she came back
He was dressed in his clothes.

The dame made a curtsey,
The dog made a bow;
The dame said, "Your servant;"
The dog said, "Bow-wow!"